Murder
at
Pullman High

John R. McLaughlin

NEWMAN SPRINGS PUBLISHING
320 Broad Street
Red Bank, NJ 07701

First originally published by Newman Springs Publishing 2021

ISBN 978-1-63692-204-1 (Paperback)
ISBN 978-1-63692-205-8 (Digital)

Printed in the United States of America

Acknowledgment

With gratitude to Ms. Nancy Baird for her assistance and helpful input and encouragement. To my son, Michael McLaughlin, for his computer knowledge; and to my daughters, Molly and Patty, for keeping me in their thoughts.

M y name is Frank MacDonald. I am fifty-six years old, about 5'11" and weigh 208 pounds. I have a lovely wife, Margaret Mary, who loves me despite my thinning gray hair and extra pounds. We have two daughters, Megan, thirty-two, who is married to a mathematics professor at Marquette University; and Maureen, twenty-nine, who was recently married to an architect who graduated from the University of Wisconsin. I met Margaret at St. Patrick's elementary school. She was in the second grade, and I was in the third grade. I was a year ahead of her. She is a beautiful woman with flaming red hair and sparkling green eyes. We went to the same high school, and after I took her to the senior prom, I knew that I would someday ask her to marry me.

I was born and raised in the town of West Allis, Wisconsin, a suburb of Milwaukee. My dad, Sean MacDonald, worked for the Chicago, Milwaukee, St. Paul, and Pacific Railroad, known locally as the Milwaukee Road. He had to quit school after the eighth grade to get a job, to support his mother, and a sister, Frances. My mother quit school after tenth grade at Mercy High School and worked in various sales positions at Gimbels department store. Her dad, Walter, also worked for the railroad, but for the Northwestern Railroad. I always felt there was some friction between my dad and Walter because they each worked for two rival railroads, so we spent little time with my mom's parents.

After my parents got married, my mom stayed home to raise my sister and me while my dad worked the swing shift as a switchman. He was in bed in the morning, when my sister and I left for school, and was at work when we got home after school. About the only time we saw him was on the weekends when we would often jump into the car and take a drive in the country. My first job, according to my dad, was to *get an education*! My second job was to see that the oil tank in the stove in the living room was full before I went to bed. There were times when my dad would wake me up at two o'clock or three o'clock in the morning and tell me that the fire in the oil stove was out. I had to get up, go down to the basement, fill the five-gallon oil can (did I mention that we lived on the second floor?), and get the fire going again. That was my responsibility, to keep the oil stove going during the cold days of winter. There were times when I wished I had a dad at home like most of my friends in the neighborhood did, but I must admit that there was always food on the table, and we never went hungry. My mom always fixed those meals in a NESCO Roaster, and the meals were always good.

In high school, I was a good, but not great, student, a good but not great athlete. I was a third-string quarterback on the football team, a third-string wrestler in the 135-pound class (behind a state champ), the third-ranked pole vaulter on the track team (also behind the same state wrestling champ). I at least had some success academically, being selected for the National Honor Society along with seven other high-ranking academic and school-involved students in a midyear class of ninety-three graduates.

After high school, I enlisted in the Marine Corps at age eighteen and went to boot camp at Pendleton outside of San Diego. When I started boot camp, I was 5'9" and weighed 138 pounds. When I finished boot camp, I was 5'9.5" and weighed 164 pounds. The drill sergeants had us running everywhere. The only time we were not running was when we were on our stomachs on the rifle range or in the mess hall eating great meals. They fed us about six thousand calories every day. When I finished boot camp, I was an inch taller and twenty-six pounds heavier, all solid muscle. I have put on some pounds since then.

During my corps career, among other assignments, I participated in the Panama invasion, the Persian Gulf War, and the war in Iraq. I had earned several military medals and citations, including the Purple Heart, which I received after an IED had nearly killed me in Iraq. Between the Panama and Persian Gulf assignments, I came back on leave to West Allis and married my best friend since third grade, Margaret Murphy. She traveled with me, lived in military housing when I was stateside, but came back to Milwaukee when I was sent overseas. The one time she traveled with me overseas was when I was assigned to a Marine station in Kaneohe, Hawaii, where our daughter, Megan, was born. When I was on assignments overseas and there was no housing available, she and my daughters lived with her parents, and Megan and Maureen attended the same schools Margaret and I had gone to as kids.

I retired from the corps after twenty-four years as a master sergeant at age forty-two. During the latter part of my military career, I had been assigned to the Military Police, so I was quickly able to get a job with the Milwaukee Police Department. I started my police career first patrolling on foot, then in a patrol car, on the south side of Milwaukee. In the years following, I rose to the rank of detective. I eventually ended up with a degree in Criminal Science and a rank of Detective Sergeant. After thirteen years, a bullet from a drug dealer left me with a choice of desk duty or a medical retirement. I chose the latter with no idea of what I would do in the future. I at least had my military retirement pay, plus the police medical retirement pay, to live on.

Chapter 1

Day 1
One Year Later

After a year of languishing at home, feeling sorry for myself, drinking too much, and driving my wife crazy, she said, "Frank, get a job, sober up, or I'm leaving."

Following a year going to AA meetings and some private counseling, I straightened up, got and stayed sober, and continued attending AA once a week. Meanwhile, I had called a retired cop friend, Carl Nelson, and asked if he would be interested in starting a detective agency with me. Carl stood about 6'2", weighed about 225, and had retired after thirty years on the force. He had once had a full head of auburn hair, which was now a thinning gray. He had earned many citations from the department, had a lot of cop friends, and like me, was looking for something to get involved in. He said, "You bet I'm interested. I am tired of sitting in a boat all day long, four or five days a week, fishing and not catching anything but small perch. But I will have to get Anne's okay."

Anne was his wife of thirty years and still a very attractive woman who kept her figure with yoga classes and swimming. They met in college her freshman year, married right after graduation, had three babies in three years, and was the love of his life. She was happy to get him out of the house also. We agreed to give it a try. We met with an attorney to get the necessary legal paperwork drawn up to get our new business started. In eight days, the MacDonald-Nelson Detective Agency was off the ground and looking for clients.

Chapter 2

Day 11

I found a suitable office space on Mitchell Street on the south side of Milwaukee, a walk-up that needed some work that faced across the street at the ancient Majestic Theater, about four miles west of Lake Michigan in a neighborhood that was rapidly changing from mostly Polish, German, and Irish residents to one of mostly Hispanic owners and tenants. The old Hills and Goldman department stores on Mitchell Street, where I had worked a few hours every weekend, had long been shuttered.

While I arranged for a sign on our door and on the street front window and some advertising in the *Milwaukee Journal*, Carl and I spent time cleaning and painting the office, getting three used desks and chairs, and advertised for a secretary. Three days later, we received a call from a Ms. Nancy Wisnewski, who said she was fifty-seven years old, a widow whose husband had died five years ago. She had retired from South Division High School six months earlier, after teaching typing and business classes for thirty-five years. She lived alone with two cats, about six blocks away on Madison Street, had never had children, and was looking for anything to get her out of the house.

When she came into the office the next day, she was wearing flat-heeled shoes, her hair in a bun, and a matronly sundress. We knew after fifteen minutes interviewing her, we had our secretary. We discussed salary, and she said, "I do not need much since I have a good retirement package from the State Teachers Retirement fund, including medical coverage."

I said, "Can you start next Monday?"

She replied with a big smile "I will be here at eight!"

MacDonald and Nelson were another step closer to getting their new business off the ground. We now only had to wait for a client to walk into our office. Four days later, Ms. Wisnewski came into the office with tears in her eyes. "Why are you crying?" we asked.

She wiped her eyes with a handkerchief and said, "I am so disappointed. I was really looking forward to this job, but I must, unfortunately, give it up. My sister, who lives in Green Valley, Arizona, has had a stroke, and I am her only living relative. I need to go see her and take care of her until she is much better. I'm afraid she will not get better, so I don't know how long I will be there."

Carl and I looked at each other, and I said, "We understand totally, and would do the same thing if we were in your position."

Miss Wisnewski said she knew of a former student named Brad Sorensen, who was one of the fastest-typing students she had ever had, and she thought he might be looking for a position where he could use his typing and secretarial skills. She wrote down his phone number, wished us a successful career, and left the office in tears. After giving it some thought, I said to Carl, "I'll give him a call and see if he is available."

I called Brad and explained the situation, asked him if he was available and interested in a job as our secretary, quoted the high praise he had received from Ms. Wisnewski, and asked, if interested, when he could come in for an interview.

Brad said he was looking for a position and asked, "Would one o'clock tomorrow work out for you?"

Chapter 3

Day 26

At one on the dot, Brad Sorensen walked into the office wearing a blue sport coat, striped tie, nicely pressed slacks, and well-shined shoes. We were impressed with the first impression he made. After introductions and before we could say anything, Brad said, "I want you to know I am gay, and if that offends you, I will understand why you would not want to hire me. I am a graduate of the Marquette School of Business and can give you many references, although my last employer fired me when he found out I was gay."

Carl said, "Brief and to the point. I like that. But what you do outside the office is no concern to us, unless it reflects badly upon us! What we want to know is if you can follow orders and be an efficient secretary. We know you have excellent typing skills and a very favorable endorsement from Ms. Wisnewski. Would you have any problems working for a couple of former cops?"

Brad said, "I have no problems with that at all."

We filled him in on our backgrounds, told him we had advertised in the paper for clients, and hoped one would soon appear. He asked if we had used Facebook or Instagram.

Carl and I just looked at each other.

"Well," Brad said, "you old reprobates have a lot to learn. Leave it to me. I will set up a website for you, and you should soon have your name mentioned in many venues."

With that, he looked at our old typewriters and asked, "Would you mind if I went shopping for some up-to-date equipment, at least a modern computer and a printer? It might cost four or five hundred bucks for some decent equipment."

Carl and I were very impressed and said, "The job is yours! Get what you need, and we will reimburse you."

Chapter 4

Day 27

Our advertising paid off. Days after we had advertised in the *Milwaukee Journal*, we received a visit at nine o'clock in the morning from a man by the name of Ralph Miller, a good-looking man, about six feet tall, well-dressed, and looking sharp. I introduced myself and my partner, Carl Nelson. Mr. Miller stated that he was the Chief Financial Officer at the Allen-Bradley Company and was the designated leader of a group of twenty Pullman High School parents, whose kids had just graduated from Pullman High School in Milwaukee.

He stated that he and the other parents felt they needed someone to represent them in working with the police and any other groups that may be involved in investigating and solving a crime. He explained that a teacher had been found murdered at Pullman and that it was his son who had discovered the body. He went on to say that many of the children of these parents had been granted athletic and educational scholarships, and they and their parents were concerned about how the incident at Pullman High might affect their future education. He was referring to a murder reported in the *Milwaukee Journal* that morning, which had been committed the day before graduation day at the school, Pullman High, where a teacher had been found dead in her classroom.

The police had already interviewed several of the students, including his son, James, and several of the children and parents whom Mr. Miller was asking us to represent. He added that he and the other parents in the group felt that the police, namely Detectives Paul Branch and Juan Gonzales, had been interviewing as many teachers and students as they could contact, with an unreasonable amount of pressure and even harassment, to find the killer or killers. Mr. Miller asked that we work with the police while keeping the parents in the group informed. He also said that money would not be a problem. I told him that our fees would be $500 per day, and if acceptable, we would do what we could, beginning immediately.

I said that we would want to meet with all the parents in the group and their kids at one o'clock that afternoon in a place convenient to him and the others in the group. He agreed and left with a promise to tell me where we would meet. I then called in our secretary, who had started that morning, and asked him to do two things: first, make up three sheets with letterheads for names and addresses for up to thirty people; second, to do the same with as many sheets as necessary for those attending to answer specific questions, which I would dictate to him.

He smiled and said, "I'm happy to have something to do again."

I then asked my partner, Carl Nelson, to ask around his old police friends to see what inside information he could come up with.

Chapter 5

Day 26

T he morning newspaper had reported that at four forty-five the previous afternoon, a student named James Miller had returned to the school after the graduation commencement ceremony to clean out his gym locker and then his hall locker. As he went by room 222, he saw a body lying on the floor with just the feet visible behind the desk. He went in, thinking that maybe the teacher had fainted. When he saw blood, he ran out in a panic, went to the main office, where he found the principal, Armando Monterey, and Jack Gray, the school security officer, and told them what he had seen.

Mr. Monterey told James to stay in the main office, called the head custodian, and told him to come to the main office as quickly as possible to sit with a student who was to wait there for the police to arrive. Then he grabbed his cell phone and headed for room 222. He found Ms. Angela Cordova lying on the floor behind the desk as James had said, checked her for a pulse, found none, and called 911 just as the head of school security, Jack Gray, entered the room.

"What's going on?" Jack asked. Then he saw Ms. Cordova's feet extending out from behind the desk. "Oh my God!" he shouted.

Principal Monterey told Jack to go down and wait at the main entrance for the EMTs and the police and bring them up to room 222. When the EMTs arrived, Gray led them up to room 222, then returned to the office to wait for the police to arrive. The EMTs checked Ms. Cordova for a pulse and found none, declared her dead, and left on another emergency call. When the police arrived, Gray led them up to room 222 and stood outside the door while they checked out the scene. The police, Detectives Juan Gonzales and Paul Branch of the Third Precinct, in which Pullman was located, observed the blood on the floor near Ms. Cordova's head and some blood on the corner of the desk. There were some books scattered around on the floor, a few on her desk, and some student desks out of order, and one tipped over.

Detective Branch got on the phone and called the coroner and said he was needed at the apparent crime scene. Detective Gonzales went to the main office and questioned James Miller about what he had observed, what he was doing in the building, and if he had seen any other students in the building, particularly on the second floor. James said he came back after the graduation ceremony to get things from his school and gym lockers and had seen no one on the second floor and just two girls whom he did not know leaving the school as he returned. Detective Gonzales said James could call his parents to pick him up and that he would like to speak with them in the main office when his mother or father or both arrived.

James's father arrived about twenty minutes later, was told what happened, and told he could take James home, but any travel plans would have to be put on hold for now. The coroner, meanwhile, had arrived, went to the scene, and agreed that the victim was dead, but he would have to have Ms. Cordova taken to the morgue to try to determine if perhaps her death was an accident or a murder. Detective Gonzales talked to Principal Monterey, asking about Ms. Cordova. Monterey said she had been teaching at Pullman for the past three years in both the English and Foreign Language Departments, two classes of English and three of Spanish, including the advanced placement Spanish class. Many of her students had passed the AP (advanced placement) test and would receive college credit their freshman year.

Detective Branch spoke with Security Chief Jack Gray in the corridor. He asked about discipline problems in the school, in general, and if Ms. Sanchez had reported any of her students creating a problem during the school year. Mr. Gray said there were a few bad apples at Pullman, but the most frequent problem was finding kids smoking in the lavatories. Very rarely did he see fighting inside the school, and those students were suspended until their parents could come to school with their child to discuss the problem. This was usually the result of someone getting jostled in the hall or in the cafeteria.

Overall, Pullman High was a good place to be a student or a teacher. He said he had been at Pullman since it opened and considered it one of the best high schools in the city and was the best he had worked in. Detective Branch took notes as they were talking, thanked him, and said, "Wait here, please. Detective Gonzales may have some questions for you, and I think the principal will also want to ask you some."

The two detectives did some more inspecting the scene, then left the school.

Chapter 6

Day 26

A fter the morning paper had been published and distributed, the police came under tremendous pressure from the Mayor, the *Milwaukee Journal,* and the school administration to solve the case. It was a difficult situation since many of the students and parents were already out of the city on vacations. When interviewed by the press, Police Chief Tom Clement, a former partner of mine and now in charge of five precincts, including the one in which Pullman High School was located, stated, "We are doing everything we can to find her assailant and will take as long as necessary to apprehend the guilty party! Please realize the enormity of the problem with the students and teachers being on vacation, spread out who knows where at this time."

When a reporter asked if the chief had any suspects, he replied, "Yes, about 1,500 of them."

Chapter 7

....

Day 26

At one o'clock, June 10 (Friday), my partner and I met with sixteen parents and fourteen students at a local church. Mr. Miller explained that one couple and their son and daughter had left on vacation right after the graduation ceremony and were unaware of the crime at the time they left. One other mother was ill and could not attend, but her son was present. One father was on jury duty and could not come, but his wife and daughter were there. One mother refused to attend and kept her daughter at home, saying that there was no way her daughter could be involved.

Her husband came alone. I introduced myself and my partner, Carl Nelson, to the group, explained the ground rules, told them what our fees would be, and set an amount that we would need to get started gathering information about the case. They, through Mr. Miller, would have to decide quickly if they wanted to retain us. At this point, I had Brad Sorensen pass out the papers I had asked him to prepare.

I asked the parents to write down their names, addresses, phone numbers (home and cell), and if they had any travel plans for the summer. I asked the students to write down where they were and with whom, on the day of the crime, who they thought might be possible suspects, including students or faculty members and any-thing they knew, or rumors they had heard that might be relevant to the crime, or if anyone had been acting strangely lately. I asked the group to talk about it among themselves after I and my partner had left, make a final decision if they wanted us to represent them, and if so, fill out the papers as requested and have Mr. Miller deliver the retainer and the completed papers they were to fill out to our office by four o'clock that afternoon.

I also said that if any of the group felt that they might have any information or special concerns or wanted privacy, they could call our office, and we would set a time to meet with them and/or their family privately. At that point, Carl and I and Brad left after asking Mr. Miller to take over the meeting.

Chapter 8

Day 26

My partner, Carl Nelson, learned through various police contacts that the coroner had determined that Angela Cordova might have been struck with considerable force and had hit her head on the corner of her desk, causing a skull fracture and severe bleeding. He also said that she was two to three months pregnant, and there were minute traces of a drug in her system, which he thought might have been a hallucinogen or a pain reliever. He would know more later.

Detective Gonzales had already interviewed several faculty members about Angela, whom among them were close to her, what they thought of her as a teacher, and if they knew of anyone who might have harbored a grudge and the names of any recent boyfriends. The teachers within her department all thought she was a good teacher and were happy to get students who had been in her classes, both English and/or Spanish. They did not know, nor were they willing to speculate, about her private life.

One of the Spanish teachers thought Angela's best friend was a hairdresser on National Avenue named Rita Sanchez, with whom she had lived for a while before getting her own apartment, and that she might know more than they did about Angela's life outside of school. They were also asked if they had seen anyone loitering around the school or anyone in school who did not appear to be someone who should be there. None did. Detective Gonzales left with names and phone numbers of everyone he interviewed should they have any further thoughts or information. Detective Branch did the same with the staff he had interviewed.

Chapter 9

Day 27

While Branch and Gonzales were interviewing the teachers and other staff members, Detective Branch had been checking his computer for background on Angela Cordova, checking her credit cards and records, even checked into the grades she had given to her students over the prior two years, looking for any anomalies that might create a reason for her murder.

He had visited Mrs. Regina Cordova, the victim's mother, to inform her of Angela's apparent murder or accidental death and to ask about any close friends Angela had, any men in her life, and any concerns Angela might have shared with her. Mrs. Cordova said, through tears, that Angela was a happy, hardworking girl and always cheerful. Her closest friend was Rita Sanchez, who took dance lessons with Angela and went out with her on most Friday nights to some Western dance places, and on Saturday, they took a yoga class together. Neither had a current boyfriend as far as she knew, and Angela had not told her about any special man in her life.

Branch decided not to tell Mrs. Cordova that Angela was pregnant. Angela had lived in her own apartment for about eighteen months now. On Sunday, she and Angela attended Mass at St. Patrick's Church, and Angela spent much of the day shopping, grading papers, and preparing for the next week's classes. Detective Branch said he would keep Mrs. Cordova informed and left after giving her his phone number.

Chapter 10

Day 27

My partner and I divided up the list of parents and kids and set times when we could meet and interview them. In most cases, we jointly interviewed the families. In some cases where the parents could only meet at the same time as other families, we would do it separately. When we were together, sometimes he would take the lead; and in others, I would lead.

Generally, we asked the family to come to our office. We would first ask if it would be all right to tape the interview, and if not, we would have Brad Sorenseni take notes in shorthand and transcribe them later. Most parents agreed to taping after we pointed out that it would help us in the process of locating the killer. At one o'clock, Mr. Miller came to our office with his wife, Elizabeth, and son, James. James repeated what he had told the police. He could not think of any student who would harm Ms. Cordova. He did not know of any problems she might have had with any other students or staff members and knew nothing about her life away from Pullman High.

While he had not had any classes with her, several of his friends did, and most thought she was a good and friendly teacher who would make herself available after school for any student who needed extra help. Mrs. Miller said most parents were worried that the publicity might affect their child's future, especially their college plans in the fall. Mr. Miller thanked us and asked that we keep him advised, and he would share any facts we uncovered with the other parents so that we would not have to talk to all the other families individually as the case proceeded. We thanked them for coming and Mr. Miller for volunteering to act as a go-between the other parents.

We spent the rest of the afternoon interviewing more families with most of the interviews a repeat of our first with the Millers. Those parents who had children in Ms. Cordova's class all felt she was friendly, very capable, gave fair grades, and was always available for a conference if requested. After the last interview, Carl and I shared thoughts but could not come up with any substantial conclusions that would point to any suspect or suspects. We then split up; Carl headed off to the local precinct to talk with the investigating officers while I went to Pullman High to check out the murder scene. Pullman High was built about 1960 and had a population of about 2,500 students. It had been named for Thaddeus Pullman, who was the Milwaukee School District superintendent, who had died of a heart attack while the school was being built.

After another high school was built, the student population was reduced to the current 1,500 or so students in grades 10, 11, and 12. Pullman was reputed to be one of the better schools in Milwaukee with about 92 percent of its graduates going on to college. Many of its graduates, since its inception, received scholarships to some very prestigious schools—some based on academics, some on athletics, and a few on ethnic-based awards. As I entered the school, I showed my credentials to the officer on duty at the front door and again to the officer in front of room 222. I looked up and down the hall and observed one door at either end, plus one double door in the middle going to the steps going downstairs. I noted that an assailant was most likely to have left through the door at the south end closest to room 222. It was the most likely route if someone had not wanted to be seen since there was a double door to the outside at the bottom of the steps there.

Inside 222, I observed a typical classroom, six rows of desks by six back. The dried blood was still on the floor and on the corner of the desk. Two of the student desks in the front row were out of line, as if someone might have fallen into them or tripped over them or backed up into them. There were about six textbooks scattered on the floor in front of the teacher's desk and another group of six stacked on the desk. Detective Paul Branch was there, taking pictures of the scene although the coroner's crew had previously done so. I introduced myself, explained who I was, and why I was there. He was friendly, shared a few thoughts, and asked if I or my partner, Carl, had learned anything from my interviews. He said he and his partner, Juan Gonzales, had been doing the same thing, probably with a little more vigorous approach. We both agreed that our primary focus was different, the police wanting to solve the case expeditiously and Carl and I wanting to see that the process was fair to the families involved.

Chapter 11

Day 27

Two things happened the next day that made the case more complex. It was stated that the door to room 222 was open when James first saw the body, indicating the killer might have left in a hurry. This would seem to indicate the killer was in a rush to leave the scene and might imply that a young person could have been responsible for what had happened. However, there should have been no students in the building since the semester had ended the previous day after the eighth period class.

The coroner's report implied the victim could have been killed one to three hours before she was found. He felt that the scattered books and chairs might have indicated that she tripped, fell over one of the chairs, hit her head on the corner of the desk, and fell to the floor, dispersing books she might have been carrying. He also stated that the autopsy indicated that she was pregnant, and the fetus was likely two to three months old. It was not possible to determine the ethnicity of the father at that time.

The second event involved a letter that had been slipped under our office door sometime that morning. The letter was from a student who said she wanted to remain anonymous. Our first thought was that it might have been from the daughter whose mother would not let her come to our parents meeting the previous day. The letter said that she had gone back to school about one thirty, half an hour before the commencement ceremony was to begin. Her locker was near room 222, but not beyond it, and she thought she had heard two people arguing and yelling in the room. But the door was closed at that time, and she could not be sure whether it was another teacher, a student, or an outsider. The persons involved seemed to be yelling in English, but she could not make out what they were yelling about. She got scared, took her books, and left the building.

When Brad Sorensen arrived, I had him make several copies of the letter. I contacted Detective Gonzales and told him about the letter. He said he would come later and pick it up, but he and his partner were on the way to talk to the coroner.

Chapter 12

Day 27

When Carl Nelson arrived, I gave him a copy of the letter and suggested that he talk to Jack Gray, the school security chief, who would normally be on vacation but had been asked to stay on duty another week. I asked him to see if he could determine which six students had the three lockers on both sides of the door into room 222. I suggested to Carl that since the letter stated that the student could not hear the apparent argument clearly, she would have been close to the room, but not close enough to hear the argument distinctly. He said, "I will check on that immediately."

Carl left, and I next called Chief Tom Clement to see if there was any more pressure from the newspapers, now gone national. He said that the papers had found out from someone that the victim was Hispanic, and he expected much more pressure from the Hispanic community, the Hispanic city Aldermen in particular.

Chapter 13

Day 27

When Carl came back with the names I wanted of the students assigned the nearby lockers, it did include the name of the girl whose mother would not let her attend the family meeting in my office. I called her father and asked that he bring his daughter, Carol O'Brien, the class valedictorian, to our office at two that afternoon and said it was important to do so. He should bring his wife too. I explained to Carl why we needed to hear her story and to expect resistance from her mother.

At two o'clock, the family arrived on time, and I asked Campbell if she had placed a letter under our office door that morning. She admitted she had. I pointed out that her locker was close to room 222 and asked her if she had heard the arguing in room 222 while at her locker. She admitted she had been at her locker then. She heard arguing, but could not tell what the yelling was about nor whether the voice was Hispanic or English. She thought Ms. Cordova might have been crying loudly.

When I asked why she did not share this information, she said she and her mother were afraid it might impact her scholarship to Harvard University. She said she felt guilty about not saying something before and started crying. I said she would be fine, but she needed to tell her story to the police. Her father said she would and asked if we thought she needed an attorney. I said it would be a good idea since she had withheld potential evidence. They all left, Carol and her mother both in tears.

Chapter 14

Day 29

Afterward, Carl and I compared notes and decided we needed to talk next to Angela's friend, Rita Sanchez. We arranged a time to meet at her apartment that evening. She said she had clientele appointments until seven o'clock but could be home by eight. She gave us her address, and we said we would see her then.

Carl and I arrived at seven fifty and waited outside. At eight, Rita had not arrived. At eight thirty, when she still had not arrived, I asked Carl to stay there, call me if she got there, while I went to her workplace. When I got there, the door was locked, the lights were off, and a sign on the door said CLOSED.

I called Carl and asked if she was there. He replied, "Nope, still waiting."

Either Rita had taken a runner, or she was in trouble. I called Detective Gonzales, but Detective Branch picked up instead. I suggested he get some cops over to her place of business and start talking to some of the locals to see where she might have gone or try to get the names of some friends with whom she might be staying. I started to worry that we might have another victim. I remembered that one of the Spanish teachers said Rita liked to frequent a bar in the Potawatomi Hotel, so I called Carl and said I was going to the hotel to see if she was there, or perhaps the bartender might remember her or some of her friends.

When I arrived, there were about twelve people sitting at tables in the bar. I identified myself to the bartender, told him who I was looking for, and he said she only came in on Friday nights, usually with a friend named Angela, but neither was there tonight. I explained who I was, why we needed to talk to her, and who the girls might have been friends with. He said they usually came in with two guys, Angela with a white guy named Tommy Thomson and Rita with a big black dude named Jackson Villanueva, a former lineman with the Green Bay Packers.

Jackson could be mean or aggressive at times but was usually cheerful, even boisterous, especially when the Packers won. He or Tommie always paid for the drinks, and Villanueva and Rita seemed to have a special relationship. He had not seen either of them for probably a month. No, he had not seen anything about them in the newspapers. He had heard about some girl being murdered, but this happened so often he never paid attention.

I left the bar and called Carl first, then Paul Branch, got no answer, then tried Juan Gonzales, reached and filled him in, and suggested they check for cameras in the hotel bar or entry to the hotel and also the desk registration to see if any of them had checked in to a room and when. They also needed to visit Tommy Thomson, an English teacher at Pullman High.

It was beginning to appear that he might be the unborn baby's father and that the voice that Campbell heard could have been Thomson's. Now it was up to the police to act on this information while he and Carl shared what they had found with Mr. Miller and his group of parents, leaving them to share it with their children, but also warning them that all of this was supposition until Mr. Thomson and Mr. Villanueva could be interviewed by the police, and until Rita Sanchez could be found. He called Mr. Miller, told them they had learned some significant information, and asked if the parents could meet tomorrow at ten o'clock again, but not to bring the children. They could explain to them at home later. Mr. Miller said he would get as many of the group as he could to be there.

Chapter 15

Day 30

At midnight, I and my wife, Margaret, were awakened by the ringing of the telephone. I answered and heard the voice of my old friend, Police Chief Tom Clement, who told me that the body of Rita Sanchez had been found in a wooded area between North Lincoln Memorial Drive and North Wahl Avenue, near the Oak Leaf Trail.

Chief Clement asked me not to share that info with anyone. He had already notified Branch and Gonzales. I said I was meeting with Mr. Miller tomorrow but would not mention this, though I expected to see it in the *Milwaukee Journal* in the morning. I knew the area where she was found because in my younger teenage days, I remembered Lincoln Memorial Drive back then as Lake Shore Drive, which ran along Lake Michigan, next to the sands of Bradford Beach where I had gotten many sunburns from my very light Irish skin and no suntan oil.

My friends and I used to swim at Bradford Beach often and would sometimes walk along the Oak Leaf Trail pretending we were in a jungle until we looked up and saw the mansions and hotels up above us. It was a long time ago! The Oak Leaf Trail was a good place to hide a body because it was sheltered by big trees and bushes and not visible to passing cars. I thought that because of where the body was found, the case might be turned over to a North Side precinct and its detectives. This case was expanding too rapidly, though at least we had two potentially guilty suspects, but it might be difficult for the cops to put a case together. I met with Mr. Miller in the morning and brought him up to date, explaining that it now appeared that none of the students were involved based on recent developments, but that the possibility still existed. I asked if he still wanted us to represent the group of parents. He said yes, at least for another week.

Chapter 16

....

Day 30

I called my partner, Carl, first thing in the morning, brought him up to date, and asked him to come in. I had something bothering me from my reading of the papers the group members had filled in at our first meeting, but I was not sure what it was. I decided to ask Carl to read through half of the student responses while I did the other half and then for us to switch our papers to see if we could spot something that might relate, which we might have missed the first time through. As I was reading the response from student Roberta Andrews, the school newspaper editor, I noticed a small article suggesting a possible drug problem among some of the students, especially the athletes and wealthier students. I pointed it out to Carl, and he said, "How did we miss that the first time through? Could it be relevant to the killing?"

I said we needed to talk to Ms. Andrews and her parents again. Then I arranged a meeting with her and her parents for one o'clock that afternoon at their home.

We arrived at the appointed time and were welcomed in. They were very curious about our visit, and I explained what Carl and I had found in their daughter's paper response, and we wanted to follow up on it just in case it might have a bearing on the murder somehow. They sat on the couch with their daughter, Roberta, between them. I reminded her of her statement that in her *Pullman Papers* article, she suggested a possible drug problem among some of the students and asked her to explain it. She said that she had heard rumors, possibly just idle chatter among kids in the lunchroom, and was just using it as a filler in the monthly *Pullman Papers*, the school's newspaper.

She thought she had heard an athlete and another student saying something about getting high. She did not know either of them and was not even sure they were talking about drugs, but she thought it might be a possibility that there was a well-kept secret about drugs being available at the school, and it should be mentioned at least. We thanked her for the information, said it might be of interest to the police, and said we would have to share this with the detectives. They should probably expect a visit from the police later.

If there was any relevance to the case, they would consider it. We asked for the name of the faculty member who was the newspaper sponsor, and she replied it was Mrs. Goodwin, an English teacher, who had been the sponsor for many years. Carl and I decided one of us should talk to Mrs. Goodwin. I asked if he would do that while I was sharing with Detectives Gonzales and Branch and Chief Clement about the drug article and our follow-up.

Chapter 17

Day 31

C arl contacted Mrs. Goodwin, explained why he needed to talk to her, and arranged a meeting for three o'clock that afternoon. Meanwhile, I told the detectives and Chief Nelson about the article and suggested it would be worth following up, especially since the coroner had mentioned drugs in his autopsy. They agreed it should be considered. I also decided to see if I could get Principal Monterey to set up an appointment with the chairpersons of the English and Spanish Departments. I wanted to get information about the teachers who worked closely with Ms. Cordova. He arranged with me to meet with Mr. English, the chairman of the English Department (I jokingly wondered if the name of the Math Department was Mr. Math but quickly threw that thought aside) at ten o'clock the next morning.

My partner, Carl, called the same evening, having met with Mrs. Goodwin. She stated that she might have missed the comment about the drugs since she relied on the student staff to check everything carefully. None had thought it worth reporting to her, or she would certainly have followed up on it. She had complete faith in the students who worked on the *Pullman Papers* and had never had any problems. She also added that Ms. Andrews was an excellent and diligent editor who had done a marvelous job as editor the past year and as a reporter in her previous three years, covering the proms, the graduations, and had good reporters covering school activities and developing the articles in the paper. She was personally unaware of any drug issues at Pullman.

I brought Carl up to date on my activities and told him to go home to his wife, Anne, and to take her out to dinner. I would call him in the morning. I also called Mr. Miller and let him know what the case status was and that we were still trying to come up with something solid without stepping on the toes of the police. He thanked me and said our efforts were appreciated, and we would be paid for all the time we were putting in. Then I went home and took my wife, Margaret, out to dinner at a Chinese restaurant. Margaret was in a serious mood. I asked her what was bothering her. She said she was worried about me and all the time I was putting into this case. She had not seen enough of me recently to let me know that I was about to become a grandpa again. Our oldest daughter, Maureen, was due in seven and a half months, and Margaret wanted to be there for the birth. I apologized and said that if Carl and I were successful with this case, it would be good for our reputation. I said that when it was settled, I would take her on a cruise to Mexico, and we would be there for the birth of our next granddaughter. It was the perfect thing to say to get her back into her normal, happy state of mind.

Chapter 18

Day 32

T he next morning, I met with Mr. English, a short, stout man who had a doctorate in literature. He said, "Call me Fred," and said he had been the department chair for the past seven years, after his predecessor had retired.

I asked him what his opinions were of the teachers in his department and if any of them might have had any negative interactions with Ms. Cordova relating to her teaching in the English Department. As several of the people involved in the investigation had done, he stated that his comments were to be kept private unless they assisted in finding the murderer. I assured him that I would share none of them with anyone but the police and my partner, Carl Nelson. He said the teachers in the department had all been there for at least ten years, except Mr. Thomson, who had just finished his second year. All performed very well and worked together nicely. Mr. Thomson was well liked within the English Department since he always volunteered to take the lower and midlevel classes, which most of the department teachers preferred not to teach. He often sought advice from Ms. Cordova in dealing with the Hispanic kids. Mr. English also stated, somewhat reluctantly, that he thought there might be more than that in their relationship in the English Department.

I asked what he thought of Mr. Thomas's performance in the classroom as well as Ms. Cordova's. Both were doing a good job, and the kids seemed to like them both. One thing that stood out about Mr. Thomson was that he often had students in after school for what Mr. English assumed was extra help. He also stated that Mr. Thomson was always impeccably dressed, drove an Alfa Romeo, had excellent manners, and was believed to have graduated from an Ivy League school. With that, I thanked him for his time and for seeing me on a vacation day.

Chapter 19

Day 32

As I drove home, I began to wonder how a second-year teacher could afford such an expensive car and dress in an expensive outfit on a regular basis. It seemed incongruous compared to other teachers who mostly dressed in casual clothing, at least the ones I had talked so far in this case. I also thought it unusual that students would want to stay after school for extra help.

When I got home, I called Carl, and we talked about it. We both agreed that Mr. Thomson and his background should be checked out. In the morning, I called Detective Gonzales, indicated my suspicions, and asked him to check into Thomson's background prior to coming to Pullman High. The fact that he was thought to be close to Angela Cordova, that he saw many students after school, that he seemed to enjoy an extravagant lifestyle, all pointed to him as a prime suspect in the sale of drugs in the school and in the murder of Ms. Cordova, and perhaps also Ms. Sanchez. Detective Gonzales said he and Detective Branch had already been looking into that possibility, and we were not to mention it to any of the parents who had hired us. He said we could tell them that their investigation leaned in the direction of a random killing by an unknown visitor at the school, possibly a prior boyfriend with a record who had been known to both victims, but not to mention Thomson at this time. He agreed to keep me informed as their investigation proceeded.

Chapter 20

Day 33

Gonzales's investigation into Tommy Thomson revealed that Thomson was a graduate of Brown University, an expensive Ivy league school, that his parents were very well off, and that Thomson had a severely retarded twin brother named William, who had died at age eleven. Tommy had always done everything for his brother, everything that William could not do himself, and his teachers in all levels of school said he was determined, from an early age, to help others who were mentally or physically handicapped.

Tommy had majored in English. His college record showed he had studied English literature, European history, Russian literature, and had one year of beginning Spanish, while also getting a degree in special education. He wanted to teach low-achieving learners like his brother, William. Tommy was successful in college, and his Alfa Romeo was a gift from his parents when he graduated from Brown University.

Detective Gonzales had interviewed Tommy several times and concluded he was a special person and not one who could murder Angela or anyone else. Gonzales also mentioned that Tommy had a friend named Manuel Delgado, who had attended Brown at the same time as Tommy on an ethnic scholarship. Manuel was also quite intelligent, but not a highly motivated student who had had several run-ins with the police during his high school and college years, but did manage to complete his degree requirements. Manuel knew Tommy from elementary school in West Allis, where Manuel had a reputation as a troubled boy, from a broken family, frequently spending time in the principal's office, and had a record as a trouble-maker when he went to Elvis Baker Junior High.

In high school, where there were many boys his size or bigger, Manuel learned to behave himself. After graduating from college, with a degree in education and specialties in carpentry, architectural drawing, and metallurgy, he was able to get a position at Pullman High as a metal and woodshop and mechanical-drawing teacher. Manuel would sometimes visit Tommy's classroom after school, when Tommy was spending time with his students, helping them with their English, as well as with other classes in which they were struggling and falling behind.

Manuel, being Hispanic, would occasionally help when Tommy's Spanish came up short. He and Manuel would sometimes head to a nearby bar later for a drink, sometimes for dinner. On occasion, Tommy and Manuel would invite Angela Cordova to come along, plus two of his other friends from his neighborhood in Bay View, Luis Hernandez and Peter Ramos. They would meet at the bar in the Potawatomi Hotel. Tommy would most often pick up the tab. On one occasion, they were asked to leave by hotel security because his friends, Luis and Peter, started smoking joints in the bar. After that, Tommy always refused to come along if Luis and Peter were going to be there.

Chapter 21

Day 34

A t this point, the investigation seemed to be at a standstill. The *Milwaukee Journal* was all over Police Chief Tom Clement and the police department, especially the detectives handling the case. Chief Clement was also giving the detectives fits for their lack of progress on the case. The detectives were struggling to come up with any kind of a lead, but without success. Who had killed Angela Cordova, and who had killed her friend Rita Sanchez? Were the two deaths related or not?

Frank and his partner told Mr. Miller that they had found nothing to indicate any involvement by the students in their group, nor were any other students found to be involved. It still appeared that the two deaths did not involve students, and the police were running out of leads. If Mr. Miller and his group wanted to end Frank and Carl as clients, they would understand. If they still wanted the MacDonald-Nelson Agency to continue to be involved, they would do so at a reduced retainer of $350 per day. Mr. Miller said that would be agreeable to him. He would try to get all the families to go along, and if any did not want them to continue the investigation, he would make up the financial difference himself. He said that since his son seemed to be directly involved in the case, if only as a witness, he wanted his son to be totally cleared of any criminal involvement.

Chapter 22

Day 34

Macdonald and his partner, Carl Nelson, met in a local tavern on Layton Boulevard to discuss, with the information they had, all aspects of the case as they saw it. Carl said, based on what he had learned in his thirty years as a cop, if there seems to be nothing obvious, then there had to be something they were all overlooking. Frank said the only thing they and the detectives had not really looked at in-depth was the possibility of a drug aspect, even though there did not seem to be any real connection to the two murders.

The coroner had said there were traces of an unknown drug in Ms. Cordova's system. There had been no preliminary report of drugs in Ms. Sanchez's system. MacDonald got on the phone, called Gonzales, got Branch instead, and asked if they had received any data on Ms. Sanchez's murder, especially if she had had any drugs in her body. Branch said they had been pretty much cut out of that investigation. I told him that Carl and I had considered the possibility that drugs might be a factor worth looking into. Branch said it might be a long shot and that he would discuss it with Gonzales and see if it might lead to anything. He thanked us and said this might be the connection that they were looking for.

Later that day, when Gonzales returned to the station, they talked about it. Gonzales got excited and said it was worth checking into since they were drawing blanks everywhere else. He immediately called Detective Phil Worthington at the Ninth Precinct, who had been assigned the Sanchez case. Worthington's boss had told them to concentrate on Luis Hernandez, Peter Ramos, and Manuel Delgado, whose names they had gotten from Gus Elliott at the Potawatomi Hotel as possible suspects. All three were considered suspects because of their previous encounters with the police in a variety of offenses, some of which involved drugs, among other things, and each had a police record. Worthington said he and his partner, Simon Garcia, would meet with Gonzales and Branch to discuss all aspects of the two cases. Gonzales suggested including MacDonald and Carl Nelson since they had first suggested the drug connection. Worthington agreed and said he would be at their precinct station at nine tomorrow morning. Gonzales called MacDonald, and they agreed to meet at that time.

Chapter 23

Day 35

T he four detectives met at nine in the morning, along with MacDonald and Nelson, and decided that Gonzales should take the lead since the Cordova case preceded the Sanchez murder. Detective Worthington said that the drug found in Sanchez was the same as the one in Cordova, but it was one that had not appeared in any other cases to date. They considered the facts and similarities in the two crimes, the relationship between the two victims, and the possible involvement of Manuel Delgado and his pals Hernandez and Ramos.

MacDonald mentioned the name of Tommy Thomson, but the detectives thought his involvement would be very unlikely, though it should be considered. They finally decided to put pressure on Delgado since he knew all the players and had a close connection to all those involved.

Carl Nelson, however, said that his instincts told him *not* to rule out Tommy Thomson as a suspect despite his do-gooder reputation. Carl felt that Tommy could have been a behind-the-scenes player had the money and the brains to be a factor in the drug trade. The four detectives said it needed to be considered, although it seemed unlikely. He did not need the money. He had an excellent reputation, had been successful in college, and was highly regarded at Pullman. There was really nothing to connect him to the drug trade.

Detectives Gonzales and Branch agreed to bring in Manuel Delgado for questioning while Washington and Garcia would concentrate on Hernandez and Ramos. Frank MacDonald said he would like to speak to Jackson Villanueva since he seemed to be one of the names that had come up early in the investigation. Carl Nelson said he would visit Mrs. Sanchez in the morning. The detectives agreed to meet again as soon as they had completed their follow-up meetings with the persons that had been named.

Chapter 24

Day 35

Nelson was able to meet with Mrs. Sanchez that same morning. He explained where the investigation stood, that they had no concrete suspect, but they had narrowed the list to a few men. He asked if she knew any of the men they were looking into. Mrs. Sanchez said none of the men were known to her, but she knew she had heard her daughter mention Manuel Delgado in her phone calls with Angela Cordova. She also remembered a mention of some famous football player, but she did not remember his name, nor did she know if he was connected to her daughter in any way. She was not aware that the girls spent time at the Potawatomi Hotel but that she had heard her daughter mention the name of Jackson Villanueva to Angela Cordova. She did not know any connection between him and the girls, nor did she even know who he was. Nelson thanked her and said he would let her know of further progress on the case. Then he headed back to the precinct.

Frank MacDonald was able to set up a meeting with Jackson Villanueva at a cousin's home in the town of Greenfield. They met at eleven o'clock that morning. Jackson introduced his cousin Henry Garcia, whose football career ended when he found out he had Parkinson's disease. He had played two years as a center for Wisconsin before the disease was discovered, but he was still a loyal Badgers and Packers fan, and now had his own landscaping business. Jackson had spent one more year playing after being traded to the San Diego

Chargers when his career ended, and he returned to the Milwaukee area. He said he had bought a 50 percent interest into his cousin's landscaping business.

When asked about his relationship with Rita Sanchez, he said they were just friends, having gone to grade school and middle school together. They would get together for drinks about once every two to three months. They always chatted about old friends as far back as fourth grade and talked about the ones they knew who still lived in Milwaukee or the suburbs. Frank asked him if there was anything more than this, a romance, perhaps. Jackson said there was none, but it might be a good idea to talk to Manuel Delgado. He said Manuel always had a chip on his shoulder and got really uptight if anyone would give a friendly hug to Rita. He always acted as if he thought he had some ownership of Rita. Frank asked if any of the group were into drugs. Jackson said he had smoked a little marijuana in eighth grade, didn't like it, and started concentrating on playing football, which did not mix with drugs, if you wanted a scholarship and maybe a professional career after that. He added that the last time they were all together, Manuel had hinted that he knew where some of the latest drugs could be obtained, but they would cost a lot. Neither he nor the girls were interested. Frank thanked Jackson for his cooperation and left.

That evening, Frank met with Tommy Thomson at Tommy's home. Tommy invited him in and offered Frank coffee or tea, or something stronger if he preferred. Frank declined, explained that the police were still following leads in the case and his role in representing a group of concerned parents and students to assure the students' fair treatment by the police. Mr. Thomson expressed his sadness at Angela's death, said he was totally shocked by it and found it hard to believe. He said they were good friends, that she helped with his Spanish, and that he and Angela would sometimes meet her friend Rita Sanchez at the Potawatomi Hotel on Friday after school. His longtime friend Manuel, whom he had known since first grade, was intelligent, but had always had difficulty staying out of trouble. However, his grades and ethnicity were enough to get him a scholarship at Brown University, which they both attended. He was surprised but happy that Manuel graduated. He became another teacher at Pullman and would often join them on Fridays at the hotel bar. He thought Manuel was attracted to Angela. He said they would sometimes meet some friends of the girls at the hotel bar.

One night, a friend of Rita's named Jackson Villanueva showed up. He was a former college and pro football player, easily excited, especially if football was on the TV. Another time, two of Manuel's other friends from the Bay View area were present, Peter and Luis. He did not know their last names, did not like them, and would not be there if he knew they were coming. He would leave shortly after they arrived if they came when he was there. He said he was there the night they all were asked to leave because Peter, Luis, and Manuel all started smoking marijuana. He concluded that though he and Manuel were longtime friends, they were no longer close friends.

Frank thanked Tommy for his time, asked him to let him know if he had any other thoughts about the situation, and left. On the way home, he had mixed thoughts about Tommy Thomson, whether he was God's gift to less-fortunate students or if it was all a façade, and he was deeply involved in the murder of the two girls.

That afternoon, Detectives Worthington and Garcia had Manuel's two pals Hernandez and Ramos picked up for questioning about the drugs found in the bodies of Angela Cordova and Rita Sanchez and also the Cordova and Sanchez murders. They were placed in separate rooms. Each was made aware of their rights prior to the interrogation.

Detective Garcia interviewed Luis Hernandez while Detective Worthington interviewed Peter Ramos. Both interviews were based upon the same set of questions but were adjusted upon the answers received. Both detectives started with the evening at the Potawatomi Hotel when the victim and her girl friend were present. Both acknowledged they had been present but left together and decided to visit another bar on the north side near Twenty-Seventh and Vliet Street, had a couple of beers, then went home. When each detective brought up the name of Rita Sanchez, Hernandez said he had never met the girl before that evening, but Peter Ramos immediately asked for an attorney, saying he was through talking. Detective Worthington had

Detective Garcia enter the room to observe and put a little more pressure on Ramos. Ramos started getting nervous and fidgety and repeated his request for an attorney.

Detective Garcia bluntly asked, "Did you kill Ms. Sanchez and hide her body along the Oak Leaf Trail?"

Ramos squirmed and said again, "I want an attorney."

Garcia said to his partner, "It looks like we got our man. Call the district attorney."

As Worthington got up to leave, Ramos said, "Wait. I want a deal."

Garcia repeated, "Did you kill Ms. Sanchez?"

Ramos said, "No, but I know who did."

Garcia said they would hold Ramos in protective custody in a cell overnight, and he could talk to an attorney in the morning. Ramos said, "I want my one phone call." He made a local call, and within one hour and twenty minutes, a lawyer named Anthony Gimelli showed up. Gimelli was considered to be connected to some *mob* members in Chicago. Detective Garcia said Gimelli could see a judge in the morning about bail but shouldn't expect it to be granted. Garcia said Mr. Ramos was about to be charged with murder and would most likely be held without bail.

Garcia immediately called Detective Gonzales and Frank MacDonald and asked them to meet him with their partners at six o'clock that evening at his precinct. He told them what had happened, including the visit from the high-priced attorney from Chicago. He thought they needed to reconsider all the events leading up to date. He also called the two precinct commanders and asked them to be present.

Chapter 25

Day 35

At eight o'clock that evening, Detectives Gonzales, Worthington, Branch, Garcia, and PIs MacDonald and Nelson met with precinct chiefs Tom Clement and Ray Adams. Detective Garcia related the day's interviews and the surprise statement of Peter Ramos. He speculated that the deaths of Ms. Cordova and Ms. Sanchez—coupled with the fact that they had unknown drugs in their systems and Ramos's statement and the appearance of the high-priced Chicago lawyer—all suggested a possible connection with a drug ring operating in the Chicago and Milwaukee areas, and perhaps including the cities in between like Racine and Kenosha.

Chief Clement said, "It all fits." He suggested it was time to get the feds involved. Chief Adams concurred and suggested that since the case started in Clement's jurisdiction, he should be the one to bring in the local FBI agents. MacDonald and Nelson were to keep this development to themselves, but at this time, it appeared there was no student involvement beyond finding the body of Ms. Cordova, and the students and their families could get on with their lives. Frank MacDonald and Carl Nelson would be out of a job, pending the final meeting with Mr. Miller.

As they were leaving, Frank told Carl his next step would be to take his wife on a seven-day cruise out of San Diego as promised. He suggested Carl should do the same, and they should all do it together. Brad Sorensen could have a one-week vacation, and when they returned, the MacDonald-Nelson Private Detective Agency would start all over, with hopefully much simpler cases in the future.

The next morning, Frank and Carl met with Mr. Miller, gave him the good news that they could all relax, have a worry-free summer vacation, and hopefully good times to come. Mr. Miller thanked them profusely and presented them with a nice check for their service, along with a very substantial bonus, and promised them that they would be sought out in the future should he or the other families need their service.

Frank went home to the welcome arms of his wife, who informed him that as soon as she could arrange it, they would be enjoying a seven-day ocean voyage to Mexico on a *Princess* cruise ship with Carl and his wife, Anne. He slept very well that night.

Epilogue

··

W hen Frank and Carl returned to their office after the cruise, they were told by Chief Clement that the FBI had broken up a big drug ring operating in Southern Wisconsin and Northern Illinois. Delgado, Hernandez, and Ramos were all headed for trial. Ramos had confessed to all the drug counts and would be getting a shorter sentence than his friends. The three had no knowledge of the killings, but it was reported a few days later that a mob member from Milwaukee had been found floating in the Fox River wearing a wristwatch that had belonged to Angela Cordova, attested to by one Tommy Thomson, who had requested and been granted a transfer to another school.

In addition to this information, they received a letter of commendation from Police Chief Tom Clement, a letter signed by the city Aldermen, a citation from the FBI, and a letter signed by Ralph Miller and twenty other parents in appreciation for clearing their children of any wrongdoing in the case of the murdered teacher. All were appropriately mounted and hung where any visitor was sure to see them.

The future looked very promising for the MacDonald-Nelson Detective Agency!

List of Characters

Frank Mac Donald	Private detective
Carl Nelson	Partner
Margaret MacDonald	Frank's wife
Anne Nelson	Carl's wife
Nancy Wisnewski	Secretary
Brad Sorensen	Replacement secretary
Ralph Miller	Parent
James Miller	Ralph's son, student at Pullman
Elizabeth Miller	Ralph Miller's wife
Armondo Monterey	School principal
Jack Gray	School security chief
Peter Gallegos	School head custodian
Paul Branch	Detective Third Precinct
Juan Gonzales	Detective
Tom Clement	Police chief
Angela Cordova	Classroom victim
Rita Sanchez	Victim, friend of Angela
Mrs. Regina Cordova	Angela's mother
Thaddeus Pullman	School's namesake
Carol O'Brien	Valedictorian
Gus Elliott	Bartender
Tommy Thomson	English teacher
Jackson Villanueva	Football player, GB Packers

Mrs. Goodwin	Faculty paper sponsor
Maureen Mac Donald	Frank's oldest daughter
Megan MacDonald	Frank's younger daughter
Mr. English	English Department chair
Manuel Delgado	Shop teacher, drug dealer
Luis Hernandez	Friend of Manuel
Peter Ramos	Friend of Manuel

About the Author

The author is a Colorado resident who grew up in Wisconsin, a 1956 graduate of the US Naval Academy, a former thirty-year high school math teacher, and a past coach of boys' and girls' soccer. He was a twenty-year member of Toastmasters International. He is the proud father of three successful children, five granddaughters, and four great-granddaughters. He enjoys golfing, swimming, dancing, and fishing.

CPSIA information can be obtained
at www.ICGtesting.com
Printed in the USA
BVHW071405160222
629137BV00001B/94